The Tale of Jemima Puddle-Duck

A Story about Trust

Retold by Karen Jennings and Mark Pierce
Illustrated by Maureen Carter

Famous Fables

Reader's Digest Young Families

All of the animals that lived at Hill Top Farm were happy, except for Jemima Puddle-Duck. Jemima Puddle-Duck was annoyed because the farmer's wife would take Jemima's eggs away and give them to a mother hen to hatch.

The farmer's wife thought, "Ducks are poor sitters. Hens are trustworthy, reliable, and they know how to sit still for weeks."

What a funny sight it is to see a brood of ducklings with a hen!

"I want to hatch my own eggs," quacked Jemima Puddle-Duck. Jemima tried to hide her eggs but no matter where she hid them, the farmer's wife always found the eggs and carried them off.

"I must leave this egg-snatching place," quacked Jemima. She decided to make a nest away from Hill Top Farm.

One spring afternoon, she put on her shawl and her bonnet and set off. She gazed at all the wonderful sites along the road, for she had never been away from the farm before. She liked her new freedom.

When Jemima Puddle-Duck reached the top of the hill, she saw the woods in the distance. "That looks like a fine place," she said to herself. Jemima landed in a clearing and began to waddle about in search of a dry nesting place. She was startled to see an elegantly dressed gentleman reading a newspaper.

"Quack!" Jemima Puddle-Duck said curiously.

The gentleman raised his eyes above his newspaper and looked at Jemima. "Madam, have you lost your way?" he asked.

Jemima Puddle-Duck thought him a very handsome gentleman with good manners.

"No," Jemima replied. "I have not lost my way. I am looking for a place where I can hatch my eggs."

"Let me help, poor duck," offered the gentleman. "You can make a nest in my shed."

As he led the way to an old shed, his long, bushy tail swept the ground. "This should suit your needs," the gentleman said.

Jemima Puddle-Duck was rather surprised to find so many feathers in the shed. But it was very comfortable and so she made a soft nest.

"I must return to Hill Top Farm for the night," Miss Puddle-Duck said to the gentleman.

"I will take care of your nest until you return," the gentleman said. "I love eggs and ducklings and will be proud to have a fine nestful in my shed."

Jemima Puddle-Duck visited the shed every day after that. She laid nine eggs in the nest. The gentleman admired them immensely. He even turned them over when Jemima was not there.

"Madam, before you begin your tiresome sitting, let's have a dinner party all to ourselves!" suggested the gentleman.

"Oh, that would be wonderful," Jemima Puddle-Duck exclaimed. "What should I bring?"

"Bring sage, thyme, two onions, and parsley," said the gentleman. "We will make a tasty omelette."

Poor Jemima Puddle-Duck. Not even the mention of an omelette made her suspicious!

Jemima quickly flew back to the farm and gathered the herbs. She waddled into the kitchen to get the two onions. Silly Jemima! She didn't realize that these are the herbs used to stuff a roast duck.

Kep, the collie-dog, met Jemima at the
kitchen door. "Where do you go every afternoon,
Miss Puddle-Duck?" he asked.

Jemima admired the collie very much, so she
told him the whole story.

The collie listened with his wise head bent to
one side. He grinned when she described the polite
gentleman with the red bushy tail.

Kep asked her the exact location of the shed
in the woods.

"Now, I must hurry back for my dinner party.
The polite gentleman will be waiting," said Jemima.

"Yes, he surely will," said Kep. He bid her farewell
and ran quickly to the village. He asked some
foxhounds to help him save Jemima Puddle-Duck
from a horrible fate.

Jemima Puddle-Duck flew to the woods and
landed opposite the bushy-tailed gentleman.

"Give me the herbs for the omelette. Go into
the shed. Be quick about it!" the gentleman ordered.

Jemima Puddle-Duck had never heard the polite gentleman speak that way before. His words surprised her and made her feel uncomfortable and scared.

Jemima went inside the shed. The door locked behind her. Then she heard awful noises from outside. There were dogs barking, growling, and howling.

A few moments later, Kep opened the door. Jemima Puddle-Duck could not see the polite gentleman anywhere. In fact, nothing more was ever seen of that gentleman again. Kep and the other dogs had chased the fox far away.

Kep escorted Jemima Puddle-Duck back home. She carried her eggs carefully in the herb bag. Jemima hatched nine beautiful ducklings and never left the farm again.

And what a wonderful sight it is to see a proud mother duck with her very own ducklings.

Famous Fables, Lasting Virtues

Tips for Parents

Now that you've read The Tale of Jemima Puddle-Duck, *use these pages as a guide in teaching your child the virtues in the story. By talking about the story and its message and engaging in the suggested activities, you can help your child develop good judgment and a strong moral character.*

About Trust

It is important for children to know they can count on others for help, love, and understanding. While we teach our children to trust, they must also learn that there are people who don't have good intentions and who may take advantage of their trust. Here are a few strategies to help your child learn the difference:

1. *Have a "no secrets" rule.* Teach your child that anyone who asks her to keep quiet about something is probably not behaving appropriately, and that it is okay for her to tell you the secret. Avoid using the word *secret* when the situation is really a *surprise*—for example, the birthday present for Dad. Children understand the difference between a wonderful surprise and a secret.

2. *Tell your child it's okay to say "no."* Assure your child that if something feels wrong about a situation, she should not hesitate to say "no" and to keep away from the person who makes her feel uneasy. Do not insist that your child hug or kiss relatives or friends if she is reluctant to do so. (She can give them a high-five instead.)

3. *Teach your child how to get help.* Your child should know how to make a phone call, and whom she can go to for help if lost or in trouble: a policeman, fireman, teacher, mother or grandmother with small children in tow, or counter employees in malls or theme parks.

4. *Assure your child that you trust her.* Be sure your child knows you will always believe her when she comes to you for help, especially if she feels uncomfortable about a situation.